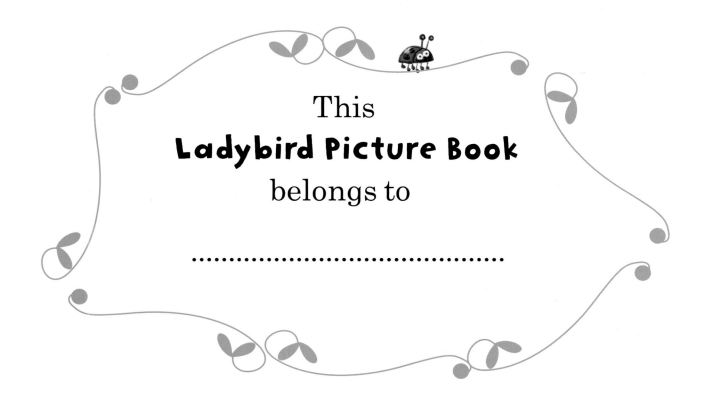

This
Ladybird Picture Book
belongs to

....

LADYBIRD BOOKS

UK | USA | Canada | Ireland | Australia
India | New Zealand | South Africa
Ladybird Books is part of the Penguin Random House group of companies
whose addresses can be found at global.penguinrandomhouse.com.

www.penguin.co.uk   www.puffin.co.uk   www.ladybird.co.uk

Penguin
Random House
UK

First published 1999
Reissued 2011 as part of the Ladybird First Favourite Tales series
This Ladybird Picture Books edition published 2019

011

Copyright © Ladybird Books Ltd, 1999, 2011, 2019

Printed in China

The authorized representative in the EEA is Penguin Random House Ireland,
Morrison Chambers, 32 Nassau Street, Dublin D02 YH68

A CIP catalogue record for this book is available from the British Library

ISBN: 978–0–241–38431–2

All correspondence to:
Ladybird Books, Penguin Random House Children's
One Embassy Gardens, 8 Viaduct Gardens, London SW11 7BW

MIX
Paper | Supporting
responsible forestry
FSC® C018179
FSC
www.fsc.org

Ladybird Picture Books

The Gingerbread Man

BASED ON A TRADITIONAL FOLK TALE

retold by Rone Randall ★ illustrated by Ailie Busby

One morning a baker said to his wife,
"Today I'll bake a gingerbread man.
He'll look just right in our shop window."

So the baker made a gingerbread man and put him in the oven. Before long they heard a noise. A little voice began to shout, *"Open the door! Let me out!"*

As soon as the baker opened the oven door,

The baker and his wife chased him down the street, shouting, "Come back here, little ginger feet!"

But the gingerbread man just ran and ran, singing,

...a hungry boy joined the chase calling,
"Come back here, little ginger face!"

But the gingerbread man just ran and
ran, singing,

...a hungry cow who said,
"Come back here, little ginger head!"

But the gingerbread man just ran and ran, singing,

"Run, run as fast as you can,

...a hungry horse, neighing, "Come back here, little ginger paws!"

But the gingerbread man just ran and ran, singing,

"Run, run, as fast as you can, You can't catch me, I'm the gingerbread man!"

Behind him chased the horse, the cow, the boy, the baker and his wife.

In the woods hid a hungry fox. He called, "What's the hurry, little ginger socks?"

But the gingerbread man just ran and ran, singing,

"Run, run, as fast as you can, You can't catch me, I'm the gingerbread man!"

No time for that!

He was just thinking how clever he was, when...

...he came to a wide, wide river.

The gingerbread man stopped. He needed to think. Up crept the fox and said with a wink,

"Jump onto my tail and I'll take you across."

The gingerbread man thanked the sly fox and he jumped onto his bushy tail.

The fox started to swim across the wide, wide river.

Very soon he said, "Little gingerbread man, you're too heavy for my tail. Why not jump onto my red, red back?"

So the gingerbread man jumped onto the fox's back.

But soon the fox said, "Little gingerbread man, you're too heavy for my back. Why not hop onto my shiny, black nose?"

So the gingerbread man hopped
onto the fox's nose.

Just as they came near to the bank, the fox tossed back his head.

And with a flick of his neck, he tossed the gingerbread man up, up, up in the air.

Then the gingerbread man fell

down, down, down...

SNAP! straight into the fox's gaping mouth.

And that was the end of the gingerbread man.

With a sly smile, the fox trotted home, singing,

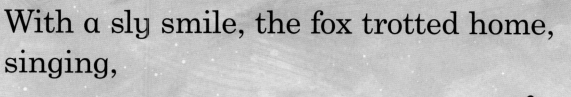

"Run, run, as fast as you can,
But **I** caught **you**, little gingerbread man!"

Mmmm!

Ladybird Picture Books

Look out for...

 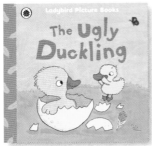 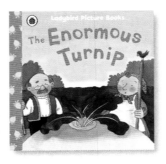  

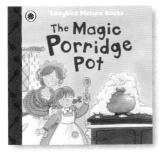    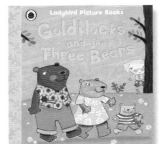

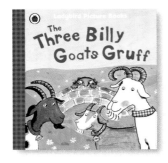 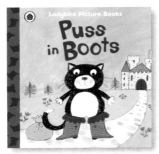   

 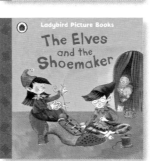